Also by Stuart Gibbs

STUART GIBBS

ILLUSTRATED BY **ANJAN SARKAR**

spy school

THE GRAPHIC NOVEL

Simon & Schuster Books for Young Readers
New York London Toronto Sydney New Delhi

SIMON & SCHUSTER BOOKS FOR YOUNG READERS
An imprint of Simon & Schuster Children's Publishing Division
1230 Avenue of the Americas, New York, New York 10020
This book is a work of fiction. Any references to historical events,
real people, or real places are used fictiously. Other names, characters,
places, and events are products of the author's imagination, and any resemblance
to actual events or places or persons, living or dead, is entirely coincidental.
Text © 2012, 2022 by Stuart Gibbs
Illustration © 2022 by Anjan Sarkar
Book design by Lucy Ruth Cummins © 2022 by Simon & Schuster, Inc.
SIMON & SCHUSTER BOOKS FOR YOUNG READERS
and related marks are trademarks of Simon & Schuster, Inc.
For information about special discounts for bulk purchases, please contact
Simon & Schuster Special Sales at 1-866-506-1949 or business@simonandschuster.com.
The Simon & Schuster Speakers Bureau can bring authors to your live event.
For more information or to book an event, contact the Simon & Schuster
Speakers Bureau at 1-866-248-3049 or visit our website at www.simonspeakers.com.
Also available in a Simon & Schuster Books for Young Readers hardcover edition
The text for this book was set in Memphis LT Std.
The illustrations for this book were rendered digitally.
Special thanks to Rob Richardson, for his invaluable help with background design,
and to Yuko Noda and Lauren Auty, who assisted with coloring and shading.
Manufactured in China
0322 SCP
First Simon & Schuster Books for Young Readers paperback edition February 2022
10 9 8 7 6 5 4 3
Library of Congress Cataloging-in-Publication Data
Names: Gibbs, Stuart, 1969– author. | Sarkar, Anjan, illustrator.
Title: Spy School : the graphic novel / Stu Gibbs ; illustrated by Anjan Sarkar.
Description: First Simon & Schuster hardcover edition. | New York : Simon & Schuster
Books for Young Readers, 2022. | Audience: Ages 8–12. | Audience: Grades 4–6. |
Summary: "Ben Ripley is recruited for a magnet school with a focus on science—
but he's entirely shocked to discover that the school is actually a front for a junior
C.I.A. academy. Ben becomes an undercover agent and goes on his first assignment
in this graphic novel adaptation of SPY SCHOOL"— Provided by publisher.
Identifiers: LCCN 2020050956 | ISBN 9781534455436 (hardcover) |
ISBN 9781534455429 (paperback) | ISBN 9781534455443 (ebook)
Subjects: LCSH: Graphic novels. | CYAC: Graphic novels. | Spies—Fiction. |
Schools—Fiction.
Classification: LCC PZ7.7.G5324 Spy 2022 | DDC 741.5/973—dc23
LC record available at https://lccn.loc.gov/2020050956

For Dashiell and Violet—S. G.

For Yuko—ごめんね!—A. S.

From:
Office of CIA Internal Investigations
CIA Headquarters
Langley, Virginia

To:
███████████████
Director of Covert Affairs
The White House
Washington, DC

Classified Documents Enclosed
Security Level AA2
For Your Eyes Only

As part of the continuing investigation into Operation Creeping Badger, the following pages have been transcribed from 53 hours of debriefings of Mr. Benjamin Ripley, aka Smokescreen, age 12, a first year student at the Academy of Espionage.

Mr. Ripley's acceptance to the academy, while unprecedented, was sanctioned by ████████████████████████ and ███████████████, Director of the CIA, as part of the operation.

As Operation Creeping Badger did not proceed as planned, given the events of ████████████████████████████████████ ████████████████, this investigation has been launched to determine exactly what went wrong, why it went wrong, and who should be terminated for it.

After reading these documents, they are to be destroyed immediately, in accordance with CIA Security Directive 163-12A. No discussion of these pages will be tolerated, except during the review, which will be conducted in ████████████████████████████ ████████████████. Please note that no weapons will be allowed at said meeting.

I look forward to hearing your thoughts.

███████████████
Director of Internal Investigations

Cc:
███████████████
███████████████
████████
███████████████

RUSSIAN EMBASSY, WASHINGTON D.C.

AMERICAN CHILDREN, PLEASE FOLLOW ME TO HALL OF HEROES WHERE YOU WILL SEE WHAT REAL LEADERS ARE LIKE...

1

CLICK!

CREAK!

CRACK!

CRUNCH!

GAME OVER

THAT SUCKS.

YOU HAVE FAILED IN YOUR MISSION. AGAIN. WOULD YOU LIKE TO TRY ONCE MORE?

YEAH. I'M GONNA BEAT YOU ONE OF THESE DAYS...

BENJAMIN RIPLEY! IT'S A SCHOOL NIGHT! YOU HAD BETTER NOT BE PLAYING THAT INFERNAL SPY GAME AGAIN!

WHAT'S THAT, MOM? SORRY, I MUST HAVE DOZED OFF WHILE STUDYING.

AGAIN*!?*

I'M TIRED OF YOU WASTING YOUR TIME PLAYING THIS SILLY GAME!

IT'S NOT A GAME! IT'S A TEST TO PROVE YOURSELF TO THE CIA. THEY'RE PROBABLY MONITORING EVERYONE WHO PLAYS TO IDENTIFY FUTURE AGENTS.

IT'S A GAME, BEN. THAT'S ALL. NO ONE'S MONITORING YOU.

HIS NAME IS BENJAMIN RIPLEY. HE'S PLAYED THE SIMULATION OVER 500 TIMES.

HE HAS STRONG MATH SKILLS, DECENT LANGUAGES—AND HE LIVES CLOSE BY.

SOUNDS LIKE THE PERFECT PATSY. BRING HIM IN.

YES SIR.

15

I ALMOST BEAT IT THIS TIME, MIKE. I WAS THIS CLOSE...

TONIGHT, I'M FINALLY GONNA CRACK THAT CODE AND WIN THIS THING ONCE AND FOR ALL...

TONIGHT? DO YOU HAVE ANY IDEA HOW MANY HOURS YOU'VE WASTED PLAYING THAT STUPID GAME?

TWO HUNDRED FORTY-FIVE.

OH. I GUESS YOU DO...

AND IT'S NOT A WASTE OF TIME. THIS IS THE CIA'S WEBSITE. I'LL BET THEY MONITOR EVERYONE WHO VISITS. IF I CRACK THIS CODE, I'LL PROVE I'M SPY MATERIAL.

BEN, YOU'RE TWELVE. NO ONE IS SPY MATERIAL AT TWELVE. YOU CAN'T EVEN OPEN YOUR LOCKER, LET ALONE HACK A RUSSIAN MAINFRAME.

I'M NOT EXPECTING THEM TO RECRUIT ME TODAY. JUST SOMEDAY. WHEN I'M OLDER.

'CHK CHK

GREAT! SO THERE'S NO RUSH. FORGET THE GAME. ELIZABETH PASTERNAK'S PARENTS ARE OUT OF TOWN AND SHE'S HAVING A PARTY TONIGHT.

WE DON'T KNOW ELIZABETH PASTERNAK.

WE COULD. MY BROTHER KNOWS HER SISTER. HE SAYS HE'LL TAKE US.

I DON'T THINK SO.

SWING!

JAMES BOND

BOND

COME ON! YOU WANT TO BE A SPY LIKE JAMES BOND, RIGHT? JAMES BOND LIVES HIS LIFE. UNLIKE YOU.

I DO PLENTY OF LIVING.

AFTER SCHOOL...

HELLO, BENJAMIN.

THERE'S NO NEED TO BE ALARMED.

MY NAME IS ALEXANDER HALE. I WORK FOR THE CIA.

20

AM I IN TROUBLE?

HA HA.

WHY? YOU'VE NEVER DONE ANYTHING WRONG IN YOUR LIFE.

DO YOU HAVE ANYTHING TO DRINK?

UH...SURE. WHAT WOULD YOU LIKE?

A MARTINI?

THIS ISN'T THE MOVIES. I'M ON THE CLOCK. YOU HAVE ANY ENERGY DRINKS?

SOMETHING WITH ELECTROLYTES?

I HAD TO DITCH SOME UNDESIRABLES ON THE WAY OVER HERE AND I'M A LITTLE PARCHED.

WE HAVE GATORADE.

THAT'D BE GREAT.

21

I GRADUATED FROM THERE MYSELF.

A FINE INSTITUTION, DEDICATED TO CREATING THE AGENTS OF TOMORROW—TODAY.

CONGRATULATIONS!

BUT I DIDN'T EVEN APPLY...

APPLICATIONS ARE MERELY REQUESTS FOR INFORMATION. AND THE AGENCY HAS ALL THE INFORMATION ABOUT YOU IT NEEDS.

FOR EXAMPLE, YOU'RE A STRAIGHT-A STUDENT WHO SPEAKS THREE LANGUAGES AND HAS LEVEL 16 MATH SKILLS.

WHAT'S THAT MEAN?

HOW MANY SECONDS HAS IT BEEN SINCE YOU FIRST WALKED INTO THE HOUSE?

842.

GLUG GLUG!

THAT'S LEVEL 16. ACCORDING TO OUR FILES, YOU ALSO HAVE AN APTITUDE FOR ELECTRONICS AND A SERIOUS CRUSH ON A MISS ELIZABETH PASTERNAK. ALTHOUGH, SADLY, SHE HAS NO IDEA YOU EXIST.

YOU KNOW ABOUT THAT?

WE KNOW ABOUT EVERYTHING. WELL, ENOUGH CHITCHAT. LET'S GET YOU PACKED. YOU HAVE A BUSY AFTERNOON AHEAD!

24

TSK. TSK. NOT A SINGLE DECENT SUIT.

HOW FAR AWAY IS THIS ACADEMY?

JUST ACROSS THE POTOMAC IN DC, BUT BECOMING A SPY IS A FULL-TIME JOB, SO ALL STUDENTS ARE REQUIRED TO LIVE ON CAMPUS.

BOURNE

Mommy's little helper

YOUR TRAINING WILL LAST SIX YEARS. YOU'LL BE A FIRST YEAR, OBVIOUSLY.

JANUARY

WHY IS THE ACADEMY ACCEPTING ME NOW? IT'S THE MIDDLE OF THE SCHOOL YEAR.

THERE WAS A SUDDEN OPENING.

SOMEONE QUIT?

FLUNKED OUT. DO YOU HAVE ANY WEAPONS? GUNS, KNIVES, GRENADES...

ER...NO.

WELL, IT'S NO MATTER. THE SCHOOL ARMORY CAN EQUIP YOU. IN THE MEANTIME, I SUPPOSE THIS MIGHT SUFFICE. JUST IN CASE.

SWISH!

I'M IN.

ASSUMING MY PARENTS WON'T MIND ME LEAVING.

ALL-EXPENSES-PAID TUITION AT A SCIENCE ACADEMY! THAT'S MY BOY!

YOU GUYS AREN'T UPSET I'LL BE GONE?

IT'S NOT LIKE YOU'LL BE THAT FAR AWAY. JUST ACROSS THE RIVER!

TAP
TAP

Mike

Hey Mike. Something exciting came up, but I want to tell you about it in person. So...

Cancel   Sen

Cancel   Se

Call me. It's important

Cancel   Send

BEEP!

Low battery

CAN I USE THIS...?

SLAM!

WHACK!

WHOA!

SLAM!

WHO ARE YOU?

MNHEM BIPPREY.

BEN RIPLEY.

I'M A STUDENT HERE.

I'VE NEVER SEEN YOU BEFORE.

I JUST GOT ACCEPTED THIS AFTERNOON.

PLEASE DON'T KILL ME.

A NEWBIE? NOW?

THIS DAY GETS BETTER AND BETTER.

YOU'RE A GIRL!

WOW. NO WONDER YOU GOT ACCEPTED. YOUR POWERS OF OBSERVATION ARE AMAZING.

CAN YOU USE A GUN?

PAT PAT

THE ENEMY INFILTRATED CAMPUS DURING AN ASSEMBLY AND TOOK ALL STUDENTS AND FACULTY HOSTAGE.

HOW'D YOU ESCAPE?

I DIDN'T. I'D DITCHED THE ASSEMBLY. ASSEMBLIES SUCK.

I TRIED CALLING FOR BACKUP, BUT THE ENEMY IS JAMMING ALL TRANSMISSIONS.

I'VE COUNTED FORTY-ONE. THEY'RE PROFESSIONAL, HEAVILY ARMED, AND EXTREMELY DANGEROUS.

I'VE BEEN HERE FIVE MINUTES AND I HAVE TO FACE A PLATOON OF DEADLY COMMANDOS WITH A TASER?

WELCOME TO SPY SCHOOL.

I JUST REMEMBERED, I CAME WITH BACKUP! ALEXANDER HALE BROUGHT ME!

WHERE IS HE?

FIGHTING THE BAD GUYS.

I THINK HE SAVED MY LIFE.

I'M SURE HE'LL THINK THAT TOO.

THIS IS THE ADMINISTRATION BUILDING. THERE'S AN EMERGENCY RADIO BEACON IN THE PRINCIPAL'S OFFICE ON THE TOP FLOOR...

IF YOU CAN MAKE IT THERE, YOU CAN CALL FOR HELP.

IF I CAN MAKE IT THERE? WHERE ARE YOU GOING TO BE?

STOPPING ANYONE FROM KILLING YOU.

PSST!

WAIT! BEFORE WE DO THIS...IS THERE A BATHROOM NEARBY?

YOU HAVE TO GO NOW?

WHY DIDN'T YOU GO BEFORE THE GUNFIGHT?

I DIDN'T KNOW THERE WAS GOING TO BE A GUNFIGHT! IN FACT, I THINK I HAVE TO GO BECAUSE OF THE GUNFIGHT.

THERE'S A BUSH OVER THERE. IF YOU COVER ME FOR THIRTY SECONDS...

HOLD IT IN, BUTTERCUP. WE CAN'T AFFORD TO DROP OUR GUARD.

TAP
TAP!

QUIET
PLEASE

RING RING RING R

RING RING RING RING

RING
RING

RING RIN

RING
RING RING

FREEZE!!

zZZT!

THIS WAS ALL A TEST?

LUCKY FOR YOU.

IF THIS HAD BEEN A REAL INCIDENT OF EXTERNAL AGGRESSION, WE'D BE MAILING YOUR REMAINS HOME IN A DOGGIE BAG.

BUT I HAVEN'T HAD ANY TRAINING YET. I JUST GOT HERE...

PAT PAT

THE SACSA EXAM IS STANDARD FOR ALL STUDENTS UPON ARRIVAL.

?

SURVIVAL AND COMBAT SKILLS ASSESSMENT.

I THOUGHT THAT TRICK HE DID WITH THE LIBRARY BOOK WAS CLEVER...

IT WAS A LUCKY SHOT.

AND USING THE TASER ON THE KEYPAD? WE'VE NEVER SEEN THAT BEFORE.

FOR GOOD REASON. IT WAS MORONIC.

I'M THE PRINCIPAL OF THIS ACADEMY. THESE ARE THE VICE PRINCIPALS...

AGENTS CONNER

AND DIXON.

YOU'VE ALREADY MET ALEXANDER HALE...

AND, OF COURSE, ERICA.

50

I THINK WE'RE ALL IN AGREEMENT THAT YOUR PERFORMANCE HERE WAS DEPLORABLE. AMATEURISH SKILLS OR WORSE IN EVERY ARENA: UNARMED COMBAT, ELUSIVENESS, SAVOIR-FAIRE...

IS THERE AN ESSAY PORTION OF THIS TEST? BECAUSE I'M USUALLY PRETTY GOOD AT THOSE...

YOU'RE NOT SO HOT ON KNOWING WHEN TO KEEP YOUR MOUTH SHUT EITHER. IF IT WASN'T FOR YOUR EXTRAORDINARY APTITUDE FOR CRYPTOGRAPHY, I'D BE SENDING YOU PACKING.

YOU HAVE A LOT OF WORK TO DO, RIPLEY.

SLAM!

YOU'RE WASTING YOUR TIME. THIS ELEVATOR HASN'T WORKED IN MONTHS.

OH. THANKS. I'M...

BEN RIPLEY. THE NEW RECRUIT.

THERE'S NO SECRETS IN A SCHOOL FOR SPIES. I'M CHIP SCHACTER. FOURTH YEAR.

I'M LOOKING FOR DORM ROOM 423.

TOP FLOOR. WITH THE REST OF THE FIRST YEARS.

LET ME GIVE YOU A HAND.

I WOULDN'T EXPECT TOO MUCH FROM THAT, EITHER.

JUST LAYER UP IF YOU WANT TO STAY WARM.

DOES ANYTHING WORK HERE?

THE RATS. SO DON'T KEEP FOOD IN YOUR ROOM.

OH. WELL, THANKS FOR YOUR HELP.

IT WAS MY PLEASURE.

ALTHOUGH, SEEING AS I DID YOU A FAVOR, IT ONLY SEEMS RIGHT THAT YOU DO ME ONE IN RETURN.

WHAT KIND OF FAVOR?

OH, NOTHING MUCH. JUST A LITTLE HARMLESS COMPUTER HACKING...

SLAM

Lock!

THE KIND OF THING FRIENDS DO FOR EACH OTHER ALL THE TIME.

?!

UH... I'VE NEVER HACKED ANYTHING IN MY LIFE...

THERE'S NO NEED TO BE HUMBLE. I'VE SEEN YOUR FILE. YOUR CRYPTOGRAPHY SCORES ARE OFF THE CHARTS.

THAT MUST BE A MISTAKE...

ALL I NEED IS SOME CLASSIFIED INFORMATION OFF THE SCHOOL MAINFRAME.

BUT THAT SHOULDN'T BE A PROBLEM FOR SOMEONE WITH YOUR MAD SKILLS, RIGHT?

WHAT KIND OF INFORMATION ARE YOU TRYING TO GET?

WHAT'S WITH ALL THE QUESTIONS?

SORRY, BUT...I JUST GOT HERE. I DON'T WANT TO DO ANYTHING THAT WOULD GET ME IN TROUBLE.

THAT'S VERY SMART. YOU KNOW WHAT WOULD CAUSE TROUBLE FOR YOU?

BEING MY ENEMY.

I DON'T WANT TO BE YOUR ENEMY.

GREAT! FRIENDS IT IS! SO LET'S GET HACKING...

CLAP!

YOU WANT TO DO THIS NOW? I HAVEN'T EVEN UNPACKED!

EXACTLY! NO ONE WOULD EVER EXPECT YOU TO HACK THE MAINFRAME THIS FAST. C'MON.

I DON'T LIKE TO BE KEPT WAITING!!

RATTLE
RATTLE

HI. I'M MURRAY...

...AND THIS IS A PORTABLE VAN DE GRAAFF ELECTROSTATIC GENERATOR.

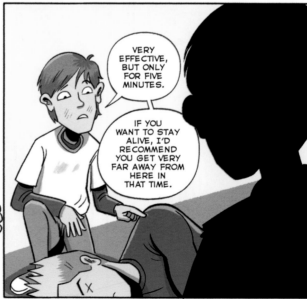

VERY EFFECTIVE, BUT ONLY FOR FIVE MINUTES.

IF YOU WANT TO STAY ALIVE, I'D RECOMMEND YOU GET VERY FAR AWAY FROM HERE IN THAT TIME.

FIRST THING YOU NEED TO KNOW ABOUT SPY SCHOOL: IT STINKS. IT HAS EVERYTHING YOU HATED ABOUT REGULAR MIDDLE SCHOOL...

SOCIAL CLIQUES, LOUSY TEACHERS, INCOMPETENT ADMINISTRATORS, BULLIES— AND ON TOP OF THAT, SOMEONE OCCASIONALLY TRIES TO KILL YOU.

YOU MEAN, CHIP WAS TRYING TO...?

ICE YOU? NO. OUR ENEMIES DO THAT. CHIP WAS ONLY INTIMIDATING YOU.

WHAT'D HE ASK YOU TO DO?

HACK THE MAINFRAME.

LOOKING FOR TEST ANSWERS, I'LL BET. CHIP HAS THREATENED ALMOST EVERYONE HERE TO DO THAT.

AND NO ONE HAS TOLD THE ADMINISTRATION?

OH, THE ADMINISTRATION KNOWS.

AND THEY HAVEN'T KICKED HIM OUT?

THIS ISN'T A NORMAL SCHOOL. WE'RE TRAINING TO BE SPIES, NOT BOY SCOUTS. YOU CAN GET AN A FOR CHEATING HERE.

SO...I SHOULD HAVE TRIED TO HACK THE COMPUTER?

HECK NO. YOU WOULDN'T HAVE GOT PAST THE FIRST FIREWALL, AND THE ADMINISTRATION WOULD HAVE BOOTED YOU.

BUT YOU JUST SAID CHEATING WAS OKAY...

IF YOU DO IT RIGHT. HACKING THE MAINFRAME IS IDIOTIC.

BUT CHIP WAS FORCING ME TO DO THAT...

AND THUS, WOULD HAVE KEPT HIS HANDS CLEAN. DOING SOMETHING STUPID ISN'T STUPID IF YOU CAN GET SOMEONE ELSE TO DO IT FOR YOU.

SLOP!

THIS PLACE IS INSANE.

THEY DON'T CALL IT AN INSTITUTION FOR NOTHING.

SPLAT!

CAN I GET SOME MEAT WITH THAT?

THAT IS THE MEAT.

GULP

62

NO ONE WILL ADMIT IT, BUT I THINK THEY MAKE THE FOOD HERE AWFUL ON PURPOSE. THEY'RE BUILDING UP OUR IMMUNITY SO THAT IF ANYONE TRIES TO POISON US, IT WON'T WORK.

ARSENIC HAS NOTHING ON THE MEATLOAF HERE.

IS THERE ANYTHING GOOD ABOUT THIS PLACE?

THE CLASSES MUST BE GOOD, RIGHT? IT'S AWESOME THAT WE GET TO TRAIN TO BE SPIES.

DON'T TELL ME YOU'RE A FLEMING.

WHAT'S A FLEMING?

SOMEONE WHO SHOWS UP HERE EXPECTING TO BECOME JAMES BOND.

WE **ARE** TRAINING TO BE SPIES...

IN REAL LIFE. WHICH IS WAY DIFFERENT FROM THE MOVIES.

MOVIE SPYING IS ALL COOL GADGETS AND CAR CHASES IN EXOTIC PLACES LIKE MONTE CARLO AND GSTAAD.

REAL SPYING IS GRUNT WORK IN THIRD-WORLD HELLHOLES LIKE MOGADISHU AND NEWARK.

THERE MUST BE SOME GOOD ASSIGNMENTS. ALEXANDER HALE DOESN'T LOOK LIKE HE'S DOING MUCH GRUNT WORK.

SURE, THERE'S ONE OR TWO CHERRY JOBS, BUT THOSE ARE FOR THE CREAM OF THE CROP. IF YOU WANT TO BUST YOUR BUTT HERE FOR SIX YEARS, BE MY GUEST.

BUT YOU'RE STILL NOT GONNA COME OUT ON TOP...

SHE IS.

ERICA? WHAT YEAR IS SHE IN?

THIRD. BUT SINCE SHE'S A LEGACY, SHE'S PRETTY MUCH BEEN TRAINING SINCE BIRTH.

THAT'S ERICA HALE.

SHE'S ALEXANDER HALE'S DAUGHTER?!

AND THE GRANDDAUGHTER OF CYRUS HALE...

THE GREAT-GRANDDAUGHTER OF OBIDIAH HALE AND SO ON.

ALL THE WAY BACK TO NATHAN HALE HIMSELF. HER FAMILY'S BEEN SPYING FOR AMERICA SINCE BEFORE THERE WAS AMERICA.

IF ANYONE'S GRADUATING INTO THE ELITE FORCES, IT'S HER.

SO YOU'RE NOT EVEN GOING TO TRY?

I USED TO BE LIKE YOU, BACK WHEN I FIRST GOT HERE. TOTAL FLEMING. THEN, ONE DAY, I HAD AN EPIPHANY ABOUT BECOMING A FIELD AGENT: PEOPLE KILL FIELD AGENTS.

ON THE OTHER HAND, PEOPLE RARELY KILL THE FOLKS WHO WORK AT HEADQUARTERS.

SO...YOU WANT A DESK JOB?

ABSOLUTELY. YOU WORK 9 TO 5, GET A NICE PLACE IN THE BURBS, PUT IN YOUR THIRTY YEARS, AND RETIRE WITH A BIG OLD GOVERNMENT PENSION.

THAT'S NOT VERY GLAMOROUS.

SO? I'LL TAKE BORING AND MUNDANE OVER GLAMOROUS AND DEAD ANY DAY.

SPEAKING OF WHICH.

THE TWO SLABS OF MEAT WITH CHIP ARE GREG HAUSER AND KIRSTEN STUBBS. THE AGENCY CAN ALWAYS USE PEOPLE WHO ARE BIG AND MEAN.

MURRAY! YOU'RE A DEAD MAN!

EVASIVE ACTION!

SPLAT!

WHO IS RESPONSIBLE FOR THIS!?

I'M GONNA GET THOSE GUYS.

I'M GONNA GET THEM GOOD.

PLEASE DON'T KILL ME... I'M INNOCENT... HELP ME, ERICA...

BIP BRROOP..ZZ

RISE AND SHINE, KID.

AHHH

HA HA HA!

OH MAN! YOU SHOULD'VE SEEN YOUR FACE JUST NOW! THAT WAS CLASSIC!

TELL ME EVERYTHING ABOUT PINWHEEL. NOW!

PINWHEEL? WHAT'S PINWHEEL?

DON'T PLAY DUMB WITH ME.

I'M NOT PLAYING! I REALLY AM DUMB! YOU SURE YOU HAVE THE RIGHT GUY?

YOU'RE BEN RIPLEY, RIGHT?

UH... NO.

DANG IT. ALL THESE ROOMS LOOK THE SAME FROM OUTSIDE.

WHO ARE YOU, THEN?

JONATHAN MONKEYWARTS.

LIE TO ME ONCE MORE AND I'LL SLICE YOU.

NOT WHERE IT'LL KILL YOU. WHERE IT'LL HURT YOU. REAL BAD.

I SWEAR, I DON'T KNOW ANYTHING ABOUT PINWHEEL.

THEN WHY DOES YOUR SCHOOL FILE SAY YOU INVENTED IT?

THERE MUST BE A MISTAKE.

I WARNED YOU ABOUT LYING...

CRACK!

AAHHH!!

DANG IT! THAT WAS MY FAVORITE BLADE!

SPIN!

72

WELL, HE WOULDN'T BE A VERY GOOD ASSASSIN IF HE LEFT A WHOLE BUNCH OF EVIDENCE BEHIND, WOULD HE?

WHY WOULD AN ASSASSIN WANT TO KILL YOU? YOU JUST GOT HERE...THEY'D USUALLY GO AFTER SOMEONE WHO WAS ACTUALLY WORTH KILLING!

SLAM

I CAME AS SOON AS I HEARD THE NEWS. ARE YOU ALL RIGHT, BENJAMIN?

YES...THANKS TO MY TENNIS RACKET.

I KNEW THAT WOULD COME IN HANDY! NICE WORK!

HARDLY. I HAVE MY DOUBTS THERE WAS AN ASSASSIN AT ALL.

I UNDERSTAND YOU'VE ALREADY RUN AFOUL OF CHIP SCHACTER TODAY.

THE ASSASSIN ASKED ME ABOUT SOMETHING CALLED PINWHEEL.

76

PINWHEEL? NEVER HEARD OF IT.

WELL, THE ASSASSIN HAD. HE SAID THAT, ACCORDING TO MY SCHOOL FILE, I INVENTED IT.

GENTLEMEN, MY TEAM CAN'T FIND ANY EVIDENCE OF THE ASSASSIN ON THE CAMPUS SECURITY CAMERAS...

HA! I KNEW IT! YOU MADE THE WHOLE THING UP!

...BECAUSE ALL THE SECURITY CAMERAS WERE PROFESSIONALLY DISMANTLED.

EVERY CAMERA ON CAMPUS?

EVERY ONE BETWEEN BEN'S ROOM AND THE NORTHERN PERIMETER. SOMEONE BREACHED THIS CAMPUS.

SOMEONE WITH INSIDE INFORMATION ABOUT OUR SECURITY SYSTEM. SOMEONE PROFESSIONAL.

AND YET, NOT SO PROFESSIONAL THAT HE COULDN'T BE DEFEATED BY A NEWBIE WITH A TENNIS RACKET.

PERHAPS THE ASSASSIN UNDERESTIMATED HIS TARGET. EVERYONE DOES IT NOW AND THEN.

HAVE YOU?

NO. BUT THEN, I'M ME.

GIVEN THE NATURE OF THIS EVENT, I THINK THE REST OF THIS CONVERSATION SHOULD BE SECURITY LEVEL 14.

YES. I THINK THAT'S WELL-ADVISED.

WAIT! YOU CAN'T JUST LEAVE ME!

SOMEONE'S TRYING TO KILL ME!

WHERE AM I SUPPOSED TO SLEEP TONIGHT?

WHERE ELSE? IN THE BOX.

78

THE BOX WAS ACTUALLY DESIGNED AS A HOLDING CELL, SO YOU OUGHT TO BE SAFE IN IT.

IT'S FUNNY: IF YOU HAD ACTUALLY CAUGHT THIS ASSASSIN, HE WOULD BE IN HERE AND NOT YOU.

YEAH. THAT'S HILARIOUS.

THESE WERE ALL BUILT DOWN HERE DURING THE COLD WAR.

THERE'S MILES OF TUNNELS. I'M NOT SURE ANYONE KNOWS WHERE THEY ALL GO.

MAKE YOURSELF AT HOME. SOMEONE WILL RELEASE YOU IN THE MORNING.

CLUNK!

I CAN'T EVEN OPEN THE DOOR?!

NOPE! NIGHTY-NIGHT!

CLUNK!
LOCK!
CLICK!

HOW DID YOU KNOW HOW TO BREAK IN THERE?

I'M TRAINING TO BE A SPY. IT'S MY JOB TO KNOW THINGS.

FOR EXAMPLE, I KNOW YOU DIDN'T INVENT PINWHEEL THOUGH YOUR FILE SAYS YOU DID.

WHAT IS PINWHEEL, ANYHOW?

I'M NOT SURE, BUT IT'S BIG ENOUGH TO LURE AN ASSASSIN ONTO CAMPUS.

SOMETHING DIRTY'S GOING ON HERE AND YOU'RE RIGHT IN THE MIDDLE OF IT.

OBVIOUSLY WHOEVER WROTE MY FILE MADE A MISTAKE...

NO, THEY DIDN'T.

THAT INFORMATION WAS PUT THERE ON PURPOSE.

83

BY WHO? THE PRINCIPAL?

POSSIBLY, ALTHOUGH IF HE DID, IT WAS BECAUSE SOMEONE ELSE TOLD HIM TO...

EMERGENCY RATION STORAGE

YOU MAY HAVE NOTICED HE'S NOT THE SHARPEST TOOL IN THE SHED...

ENTER CODE

THE GUY'S HAD A BIT OF A TORTURED PAST.

WHAT HAPPENED TO HIM?

HE WAS TORTURED.

A LOT.

EVERY TIME HE WENT INTO THE FIELD, HE GOT CAUGHT.

HE WASN'T A VERY GOOD SPY.

SO THE CIA PUT HIM IN CHARGE OF THE SPY SCHOOL?

YOU CAN'T HAVE AN IDIOT LIKE THAT OUT IN THE FIELD. IT'D BE A DISASTER. MOST LIKELY, THE CIA KNOWS HE'S A BONEHEAD.

DRIED PEAS

THEY JUST WANT SOMEONE WHO WON'T QUESTION ORDERS.

DRIED PEAS

LIKE FUDGING YOUR FILE TO HELP TRACK DOWN A MOLE.

SO HE PUTS IN FALSE INFORMATION, IT LEAKS TO THE BAD GUYS, THE BAD GUYS COME AFTER ME, AND...

OH NO! I'M THE BAIT?

EXACTLY. YOU WERE BROUGHT IN AS PART OF OPERATION CREEPING BADGER.

CREEPING BADGER?

THEY USED UP ALL THE GOOD NAMES FOR MISSIONS BACK IN THE SIXTIES. CONSIDER YOURSELF LUCKY. THE LAST MISSION HERE WAS RANCID EARWIG.

YOU GONNA BARF?

I'M JUST FEELING A BIT OVERWHELMED. AND HUNGRY. I HAD TO RUN FOR MY LIFE BEFORE I FINISHED DINNER.

GURGLE

IF I WAS ONLY BROUGHT IN AS BAIT... AM I EVEN QUALIFIED TO GO TO THIS SCHOOL?

NO. I THINK THEY PICKED YOU BECAUSE YOU LOOK GOOD ON PAPER. AND YOU LIVE CLOSE BY, SO THEY DIDN'T HAVE TO SPRING FOR AIRFARE.

SO, WHAT'S THEIR PLAN FOR WHEN I SURVIVE? KICK ME OUT AND SEND ME BACK TO REGULAR SCHOOL?

OH, THEY CAN'T DO THAT. YOU KNOW THE ACADEMY EXISTS. FRANKLY, I DON'T THINK ANYONE EXPECTED YOU TO SURVIVE THIS LONG.

EVEN YOUR FATHER? HE RECRUITED ME.

HE MUST HAVE BEEN GIVEN SOME INTELLIGENCE ON THIS.

MUNCH! MUNCH!

MY FATHER DOESN'T HAVE AS MUCH INTELLIGENCE AS YOU'D THINK.

DOES THAT TASTE FUNNY TO YOU?

86

SHOULD IT?

POSSIBLY. IT'S BEEN DOWN HERE FOR SIXTY YEARS.

MY FATHER **WAS** ONE OF THE FEW PEOPLE WITH ACCESS TO YOUR FILE, THOUGH.

BLEURGH!

AND THE ASSASSIN MUST HAVE BEEN IN CONTACT WITH ONE OF THEM, BECAUSE HE KNEW ABOUT PINWHEEL.

THE PRINCIPAL ALSO HAD THE FILE...

SO DID CHIP SCHACTER. THAT'S WHY HE THOUGHT I COULD HACK THE SCHOOL MAINFRAME.

THAT IDIOT. IT'S ALMOST IMPOSSIBLE TO HACK THE SCHOOL MAINFRAME.

WE NEED TO GET A LIST OF EVERYONE WHO WAS GIVEN A COPY OF YOUR FILE.

HOW?

WE'LL HAVE TO HACK THE SCHOOL MAINFRAME.

YOU JUST SAID THAT WAS IMPOSSIBLE!

NO, I SAID ALMOST IMPOSSIBLE. THERE'S A DIFFERENCE.

ARE YOU EVEN SUPPOSED TO BE INVESTIGATING THIS?

LET'S CONSIDER THIS AN EXTRA-CREDIT ASSIGNMENT FOR BOTH OF US.

US?

YOU THINK I WENT THROUGH ALL THE TROUBLE TO SNEAK INTO THE BOX AND DISCUSS THIS WITH YOU FOR FUN? TO FIND THE MOLE, I NEED YOUR HELP.

WON'T THAT BE DANGEROUS?

EXTREMELY. BUT IF YOU HELP ME CATCH THEM, YOU'LL PROVE YOUR WORTH TO THE SCHOOL.

SO ARE YOU WITH ME?

THE MAINFRAME SERVERS ARE ALL DEEP UNDERGROUND IN AN IMPENETRABLE VAULT.

AND EVEN IF WE COULD PENETRATE IT, WE CAN'T HACK THEM.

SO WE TARGET THE WEAKEST LINK IN ANY COMPUTER'S SYSTEM...

THE HUMAN ONE.

THE PRINCIPAL KNOWS HOW TO ACCESS THE SERVER.

SO WE USE HIM.

NO WAY! WHAT'D YOU DO?

TALKED. FOR HOURS. SHE HAS A PROJECT SHE WANTS ME TO WORK ON WITH HER.

LIKE WHAT? SOME KIND OF BORING COMPUTER CODING THING?

IT'S A LITTLE MORE INTERESTING THAN THAT.

SOUNDS COOL.

OH, IT IS. I GOTTA GO.

SEND ME A PHOTO!

CLICK!

TIME FOR SPY SCHOOL!

IF YOU WANT TO AVOID NINJAS... THE FIRST STEP IS...STAY OUT OF JAPAN.

IF CRANDALL CATCHES YOU SLEEPING, HE'LL SPRING A POP QUIZ ON YOU.

TAP TAP!

TRY THESE.

ARE ALL CLASSES HERE THIS BORING?

NO. THE OTHERS ARE SADISTIC, PAINFUL, AND POTENTIALLY LIFE-THREATENING.

SO ENJOY THIS ONE. CATCH UP ON YOUR SLEEP.

IF WE COULD WEAPONIZE CRANDALL'S LECTURES, WE'D NEVER HAVE TO WORRY ABOUT OUR ENEMIES AGAIN. WE COULD JUST BORE THEM ALL TO DEATH.

STEP TWO IS STAY FAR FROM THE SEA.

WAIT. THAT'S HOW YOU AVOID VIKINGS.

HI!

DID YOU REALLY FIGHT OFF AN ASSASSIN IN YOUR ROOM LAST NIGHT?

UH...YEAH.

AWESOME! IS THAT WHY THEY RECRUITED YOU? BECAUSE YOU'RE A MARTIAL ARTS EXPERT?

NO. I'M JUST GOOD AT MATH.

RIGHT. EVERYONE'S HEARD THAT. BUT IT'S A SMOKESCREEN, RIGHT?

BECAUSE THE MATHLETES AROUND HERE COULDN'T FIGHT OFF A MOSQUITO.

I'M ZOE, BY THE WAY.

SHAKE

NICE HANDS. CAN YOU KILL WITH THEM?

MAYBE.

HA HA HA

98

99

YOU GUYS ARE IDIOTS.

LAST NIGHT WAS ALL FAKE. CHIP TOLD ME. I MEAN, LOOK AT THIS GUY.

HE'S A WIMP. IF THAT HAD BEEN A REAL ASSASSIN, HE'D BE DEAD.

IF IT WAS FAKE, WHY'D THE ADMINISTRATION GO TO DEFCON 4? TRUST ME, BEN'S THE REAL DEAL. HE COULD MOP THE FLOOR WITH YOU.

THEN MAYBE HE AND I SHOULD PUT THAT TO THE TEST. RIGHT AFTER CLASS.

YOU'RE ON!

THE YOUNG AGENT FINALLY AWAKENS!

I REMEMBER THE FIRST TIME I WAS ATTACKED BY NINJAS. NORTH KOREA. MY MARTIAL ARTS SKILLS WEREN'T WHAT THEY ARE NOW...

BUT THANKFULLY, THERE WERE ONLY TWO OF THEM AND I HAD AN EXPLODING BELT BUCKLE.

HOW LONG HAVE I BEEN UNCONSCIOUS?

ABOUT TEN HOURS.

THAT LONG? SHOULDN'T I BE IN A HOSPITAL?

105

FOR A LITTLE BUMP? THAT'S NOTHING. ONE TIME, IN AFGHANISTAN, I WAS UNCONSCIOUS FOR EIGHT DAYS.

GLUG GLUG!

WHERE AM I?

THE EAGLE'S NEST. A TOP-SECRET PIED-À-TERRE I KEEP ON CAMPUS FOR WHEN A SITUATION DEMANDS MY ATTENTION. LIKE NOW.

YOU'RE HERE TO FIND THE MOLE?

LEARNED ABOUT THE MOLE, DID YOU? I KNEW YOU WERE SMART. I THINK YOU MIGHT BE OF SERVICE ON MY MISSION.

YOU WANT MY HELP?

YES. ALTHOUGH NO ONE ELSE CAN KNOW YOU'RE HELPING ME.

NOT EVEN ERICA?

I'LL ADMIT, ERICA IS AN EXCELLENT STUDENT. I'VE TAUGHT HER QUITE A LOT OVER THE YEARS. BUT I'M NOT SURE SHE'S READY FOR THIS.

AND YOU THINK I AM?

YOU DON'T REALLY HAVE A CHOICE. YOU'RE IN THE THICK OF THIS...

SO FOR NOW, IT WILL BE JUST THE TWO OF US, MATCHING WITS AGAINST THIS NEFARIOUS MENACE...

DING!

OOH! MY HOT POCKETS ARE READY!

I ASSUME YOU'RE HUNGRY.

SLIDE

KNIFE... KNIFE

SO...DO YOU HAVE ANY LEADS AS TO WHO THE MOLE IS?

OF COURSE! ALTHOUGH RIGHT NOW, I'D LIKE TO KNOW WHO YOU THINK IT IS.

MAYBE CHIP SCHACTER? HE KNEW ABOUT MY FAKE CRYPTOGRAPHY SKILLS RIGHT AWAY. WHICH MEANS HE MUST HAVE READ MY FILE.

EXCELLENT DEDUCTION! ANYONE ELSE?

GREG HAUSER OR KIRSTEN STUBBS? THEY LOOK LIKE CHIP'S FOLLOWERS, BUT MAYBE ONE OF THEM IS REALLY THE BRAINS.

HMMM. VERY INTRIGUING. I LIKE HOW YOU THINK, BENJAMIN. YOU REMIND ME OF A YOUNG ME.

BEEP! BEEP! BEEP!

OH DEAR. LOOKS LIKE I HAVE A SMALL CRISIS TO ATTEND TO. I'LL HAVE TO CUT THIS SHORT.

AND I NEED TO BLINDFOLD YOU BEFORE YOU LEAVE. THE LOCATION OF THE EAGLE'S NEST IS CLASSIFIED.

SO...WHAT DO WE DO ON OUR MISSION?

CLUNK!

SWING!

YOU KEEP A CLOSE EYE ON CHIP AND HIS GOONS. I'LL SEE WHAT I CAN DIG UP ON THEM.

BUT WE MUST STAY ALERT AT ALL COSTS. OUR LIVES HANG IN THE BALANCE!

ANY LAPSE IN AWARENESS COULD LEAD TO...

...DISASTER.

PHEW

MUNCH MUNCH

CLICK!

AHHHHHH!!

OUCH!

SLAM!

OOOFF!!

Delman's
Basics of
Cryptography

ANGRY MONKEY!

CLAP!

DEADLY COBRA!

WILD STALLION!

RIPLEY, I HAVE A SPECIAL MOVE I'VE COME UP WITH ESPECIALLY FOR YOU: THE BASHFUL ARMADILLO.

WHAT'S THAT?

IT'S WHERE YOU CURL IN A BALL, PROTECT YOUR SOFT BITS, AND HOPE SOMEONE SAVES YOUR BACON BEFORE YOU'RE BEATEN TO DEATH!

RIPLEY'S THE MOST PATHETIC FLEMING EVER. HE MUST HAVE BEEN RECRUITED BY MISTAKE.

NO WAY. HE'S FAKING IT. NO ONE COULD POSSIBLY BE THAT BAD UNLESS THEY WERE TRYING TO.

BOOM!

QUIET!

MATH TEST IN PROGRESS

FLIP!

118

THANKS.

ARE YOU OUT HERE SOLO?

I'M TEAMED UP WITH CHAMELEON. HE'S DOING RECON ON THE ENEMY.

HE OUGHT TO BE BACK BY NOW.

PAT PAT

I'M HERE.

AAAAAAAAA!!

AAAAA...AAAMAZING WORK. I ALMOST DIDN'T EVEN NOTICE YOU.

GREAT NEWS, CHAMELEON! SMOKESCREEN'S JOINING UP WITH US!

GEE, THAT'S GREAT.

WHAT'D YOU LEARN ON RECON?

THE ENEMY HAS THEIR FLAG SET UP AT THE OLD MILL. ONE GUARD AT EACH CORNER AND BULL'S-EYE BAILEY'S UP ON THE ROOF.

BULL'S-EYE? UGH. HE'S THE BEST SNIPER AT SCHOOL.

124

HAS EITHER OF YOU SEEN ERICA? MAYBE WE COULD TEAM UP WITH HER.

ICE QUEEN? FORGET IT. SHE DOESN'T WORK WITH ANYONE ELSE OR EVEN LIKE ANYONE ELSE.

SHE LIKED JOSHUA HALLAL...

WHO'S THAT?

NO ONE TOLD YOU ABOUT HIM? HE WAS A COUPLE YEARS OLDER THAN US. TOP OF HIS CLASS.

UNTIL HE GOT ASSASSINATED.

ASSASSINATED?! HOW?!

WE DON'T KNOW. THE ADMINISTRATION COVERED IT UP. I DON'T THINK ANYONE EVEN KNOWS WHO DID IT.

WHEN DID THIS HAPPEN?

ONLY A FEW DAYS BEFORE THEY BROUGHT YOU IN.

ALEXANDER SAID THERE WAS A SUDDEN OPENING. THAT SOMEONE FLUNKED OUT.

TECHNICALLY, THAT'S TRUE. IF YOU DIE HERE, THEY FLUNK YOU POSTHUMOUSLY.

FOR FAILING TO STAY ALIVE.

SHHHH! WE'RE HERE!

10 MINUTES LATER...

CAN YOU HIT BULL'S-EYE FROM HERE?

I'M MORE OF A HAND-TO-HAND COMBAT KIND OF GUY.

CLICK!

RIGHT! WHILE I HIT BULL'S-EYE, YOU CAN RUN DOWN AND TAKE OUT EVERYONE ELSE AT CLOSE RANGE.

GOOD PLAN.

CRACK!

WHAT THE??

CLICK!

WHO IS IT?

IT'S CHIP AND HAUSER. LOOKS LIKE THEY'RE UP TO SOMETHING.

IF IT'S NOT PART OF THE GAME, IT'S NOT IMPORTANT. OUR GRADES ARE ON THE LINE HERE. CHAMELEON'S GONNA MARTYR HIMSELF IN TWO MINUTES...

WHOOP WHOOP!

BANG!

SPLAT!

BANG!

SPLAT!

SPLAT!

BANG!

SPLAT!

BANG!

...UNLESS HE SYNCHRONIZED HIS WATCH WRONG.

OH MAN! THEY SMURFED HIM!

SPLAT!

SPLAT!

BANG!
BANG!

HOORAY!

WAY TO GO, ERICA!!

WOOHOO!

PROFESSOR SPIKES GAVE ME A D IN HISTORY OF SPYING. JUST BECAUSE I DIDN'T KNOW WHEN THE WAR OF 1812 TOOK PLACE...

WE'RE HERE! CHECK IT OUT!

POWDERED EGGS

CLANK!

YOU CAN RUN, BUT YOU CAN'T HIDE!

EXIT

SLAM!

143

I DON'T CARE! FIGHTING IS NOT ALLOWED AT THIS ACADEMY!

BUT WE FIGHT ALL THE TIME IN CLASS.

THAT'S FOR A GRADE! UNSANCTIONED FIGHTING IS DIFFERENT. BOTH OF YOU, IN MY OFFICE NOW!

OOOH!

OOOH!

OOOH!

145

147

YOU'RE IN THE PERFECT SPOT TO MOVE OUR INVESTIGATION FORWARD. I NEED YOU TO DO TWO THINGS.

FIRST, PAY CLOSE ATTENTION TO EVERYTHING THE PRINCIPAL DOES.

DON'T TAKE YOUR EYES OFF HIM. SECOND, I NEED YOU TO INSULT HIM.

YES, INSULT HIM. I NEED YOU TO TRUST ME. YOU'LL BE OKAY.

...WHEN I WAS A STUDENT HERE, WE KNEW HOW TO BEHAVE. WOULD YOU LIKE TO KNOW WHAT THE PUNISHMENT FOR FIGHTING WAS BACK THEN?

WAS IT THE STOCKADE? THEY USED THAT A LOT BACK IN COLONIAL AMERICA.

WHAT DID YOU JUST SAY?

THAT YOU'RE OLD. WAS I BEING TOO SUBTLE FOR YOU?

THAT'S PERFECT! KEEP IT UP!

ARE YOU LOOKING FOR AN EVEN WORSE PUNISHMENT? BECAUSE I'M HAPPY TO GIVE IT TO YOU.

WHATEVER IT IS, IT CAN'T BE WORSE THAN YOUR BREATH.

WHAT'D YOU HAVE FOR LUNCH TODAY, DOG TURDS?

THAT'S IT! I'M PUTTING YOU ON TOTAL PROBATION!

GREAT! MAKE HIM DO IT NOW.

FINE. LET'S DO IT NOW.

RIGHT NOW?

RIGHT NOW.

RIGHT NOW.

YOU MESS WITH THE BULL—AND YOU GET THE HORNS.

THAT'S FUNNY. WHEN I LOOK AT YOU, I THINK OF THE OTHER END OF THE BULL.

WHOA THERE, TIGER. TAKE IT EASY. JOB'S DONE.

YOU DON'T THINK I CAN GET TOUGHER? FROM NOW ON, YOU'RE SLEEPING IN THE BOX.

BUT... I'M ALREADY SLEEPING THERE.

WHAT IDIOT PUT YOU IN THE BOX?

UH... YOU DID.

AN ASSASSIN TRIED TO KILL ME IN MY ROOM, REMEMBER? SO YOU SENT ME TO THE BOX FOR MY SAFETY!

AND YOU'RE STILL THERE?

NO ONE EVER TOLD ME I COULD LEAVE.

WELL YOU CAN'T! BUT NOT BECAUSE OF YOUR SAFETY!

FOR INSUBORDINATION!

SLAM
WAAWAA

WAAWAA WAAWAA WAAWAA

SIR, THAT BUTTON IS ONLY SUPPOSED TO BE USED FOR EMERGENCIES.

THIS IS AN EMERGENCY! THIS BOY'S BEHAVIOR HAS BEEN DOWNRIGHT MUTINOUS! ESCORT HIM TO THE BOX!

MARK MY WORDS, RIPLEY. YOU WILL RUE THE DAY YOU MET ME.

I ALREADY DO.

154

YOU MIGHT BE A FRAUD AND A LIAR, BUT YOU HAVE SOME SERIOUS GUTS.

THANKS.

THOUGH YOU'D STILL BETTER KEEP YOUR MOUTH SHUT ABOUT YOU-KNOW-WHAT.

THANKS! YOU TWO HAVE A NICE NIGHT YOURSELVES!

ERICA, WHATEVER I JUST DID BETTER BE WORTH IT. I'M IN SERIOUS TROUBLE WITH THE SCHOOL BULLY AND THE PRINCIPAL.

ERICA?

HELLO?

COME IN ERICA...

IT'S MIKE! ELIZABETH PASTERNAK IS HAVING ANOTHER PARTY TOMORROW NIGHT AND THIS TIME, YOU'RE GOING. LET ME KNOW WHAT TIME TO SPRING YOU FROM NERD SCHOOL!

TAP
TAP

Would love for you to spring me tomorrow. FYI, you'll need a commando team and a getaway car.

SEND | CANCEL

CLICK!

TOSS!

SKYFALL

SKYFALL

157

DID YOU FIND THE BOMB?

NO.

YOU MEAN IT'S STILL DOWN HERE?!

KEEP YOUR PANTIES ON. I COULDN'T FIND IT BECAUSE IT'S NOT HERE ANYMORE.

MAYBE YOU MISSED IT. THIS ONE WAS BACK IN SOME PIPES...

...I KNOW. I FOUND WHERE THE BOMB WAS. BUT ALL THAT WAS LEFT WAS THE RESIDUE OF SOME C4 PUTTY AND A WHIFF OF CHIP SCHACTER'S TOXIC AFTERSHAVE. THAT'S WHAT YOU WERE FIGHTING ABOUT? YOU SAW HIM WITH IT?

HIM AND HAUSER. THEY CAME IN THROUGH A SECRET ENTRANCE WHILE...

...I WAS CAPTURING THE FLAG. I SAW YOU GOING AFTER THEM.

THROUGH A SNOWSTORM? WHILE YOU WERE FIGHTING A DOZEN ENEMIES?

I'M GOOD AT MULTITASKING.

WHY DIDN'T YOU FOLLOW US, THEN?

I HAD TO GO GET THE TRANSMITTER SO I COULD PLANT IT ON YOU WHEN YOU GOT BUSTED FOR FIGHTING.

DON'T YOU MEAN IF I GOT BUSTED FOR FIGHTING?

NO. I FIGURED THERE WAS AN EXTREMELY GOOD CHANCE CHIP WOULD SPOT YOU AND TRY TO KICK YOUR BUTT.

SO DO YOU THINK CHIP CAME BACK AND REMOVED THE BOMB?

I DOUBT IT. CHIP GOT A D-MINUS ON BOMB DEFUSION LAST SEMESTER.

161

IF CHIP IS SO BAD WITH BOMBS, HE PROBABLY DIDN'T PLANT THAT ONE EITHER.

YOU THOUGHT HE DID?

ER...YES. HE'S A BULLY.

BULLIES HANG YOU FROM THE FLAGPOLE BY YOUR UNDERWEAR. THEY DON'T BLOW UP SCHOOLS.

SO HOW'D HE KNOW ABOUT THE BOMB?

DON'T KNOW. MAYBE HE JUST STUMBLED ACROSS IT. THERE'S A FEW MORE PRESSING QUESTIONS, THOUGH.

163

LIKE: WHO PUT THE BOMB DOWN THERE IF CHIP DIDN'T?

YES, LIKE THAT. ALSO: WHY WAS THE BOMB DOWN THERE IN THE FIRST PLACE? IT WASN'T NEAR ANYTHING IMPORTANT. JUST STORAGE FOR THE CAFETERIA.

MAYBE THE BOMBER WAS ONLY LOOKING TO SEND A MESSAGE.

WHAT KIND OF MESSAGE WOULD BLOWING UP A BUNCH OF CANNED PEAS SEND?

UM...STOP SERVING US CANNED PEAS?

I THINK YOU COULD GET THAT POINT ACROSS WITH AN EMAIL.

YOU KNOW HOW TO USE A GRAPPLING HOOK, RIGHT?

OH YEAH. WE HAD A WHOLE CLASS IN GRAPPLING HOOK USAGE BACK AT MY NORMAL MIDDLE SCHOOL.

GREAT. FIRE THIS UP TO THE ROOF.

DOFF!

COULDN'T WE CHECK THE CAMERAS IN THE TUNNELS TO SEE IF THE BOMBER IS ON THEM?

I ALREADY DID. THE CAMERAS WERE DISMANTLED.

CLICK!

WIZZ!!

WOOSH!

CLUNK!

LIKE I SAID, THIS ISN'T GOING TO BE EASY. THE ACCESS CODE HAS SIXTEEN-BIT DAISY-CHAIN ENCRYPTION ON IT.

WHAT IS THAT, ANYWAY?

CREAK!

HAVEN'T YOU READ DELMAN'S *BASICS OF CRYPTOGRAPHY* YET?

I KEEP TRYING TO. BUT THAT BOOK IS MIND-NUMBING. READING IT IS LIKE INHALING CHLOROFORM.

YOU'VE OBVIOUSLY NEVER INHALED CHLOROFORM.

THE DAISY CHAIN IS A SIXTEEN-CHARACTER CODE RANDOMLY SELECTED BY A CIA COMPUTER...

EACH DAY, THE NEXT DAY'S CODE IS SENT IN AN ENCRYPTED EMAIL TO EVERYONE'S ACCOUNT.

THEN, IN THEORY, YOU'RE SUPPOSED TO COMMIT IT TO MEMORY.

BUT THE PRINCIPAL DOESN'T?

THAT'S MY ASSUMPTION—GIVEN THAT THE PRINCIPAL IS AN IDIOT...

THINK BACK TO THIS AFTERNOON. WHAT DID HE DO BEFORE HE LOGGED IN?

THAT'S WHY YOU HAD ME INSULT HIM? TO GET HIM TO LOG IN?

YES. SO TELL ME: WHAT'D HE DO?

SPIN!

HMMM...

HOLD ON. I'M WORKING ON IT. C'MON, BEN, THINK!

UM...DIDN'T YOU SAY YOU WERE GOING TO GIVE ME A HUG?

YES. BUT I DIDN'T SAY WHEN.

OH. I WAS KIND OF ASSUMING IT'D BE NOW.

WHICH WAS A MISTAKE. POOR NEGOTIATING ON YOUR PART.

HERE WE GO!

EVERYONE WHO RECEIVED A PERSONAL COPY OF YOUR FILE.

DIRECTOR OF THE CIA, A COUPLE OTHER MUCKETY-MUCKS, SOME PROFESSORS, MY FATHER...

AUTHORIZED

DANIEL CON
PATRICIA DIX
ALEXANDER HAL
DEREK FORSHAW
US CRANDALL
NABUS SIDEBOT
CUEVO

PROFESSOR CRANDALL? WHO'D TRUST HIM WITH ANYTHING CLASSIFIED? AND WHO'S BARNABUS SIDEBOTTOM?

YOU'RE IN HIS OFFICE RIGHT NOW.

DANIEL CONNER
PATRICIA DIXON
ALEXANDER HALE
DEREK FORSHAW
LUCAS CRANDALL
BARNABUS SIDEBOTTOM
TINA CUEVO

TINA CUEVO? SHE'S ONLY A STUDENT.

BUT SHE WAS SUPPOSED TO BE YOUR RESIDENT ADVISER...UNTIL YOU ENDED UP IN THE BOX. SO SHE HAD TO KNOW ABOUT YOU.

OKAY. TIME FOR PHASE TWO.

✉ Compose Email

To:
Cc:
Bcc: undisclosed recipients

With regard to recent development concerning academy student Benjamin Ripley, I am requesting a

TAP TAP TAP

THINK CHIP GOT MY FILE FROM TINA?

NO WAY. TINA'S RANKED THIRD IN HER CLASS. SHE WOULD NEVER SHARE CLASSIFIED INFORMATION.

MAYBE SHE ACCIDENTALLY LEFT IT WHERE HE COULD ACCESS IT.

OTHER HAND.

RIP!

WE'RE DONE HERE. LET'S GO.

WHAT'S JACKHAMMER?

THE ULTIMATE CODEBREAKER.

ABLE TO DEMOLISH ANY ENCRYPTION.

A TOTAL GAME CHANGER.

CLICK!

SO IF ANYONE WANTS TO GET JACKHAMMER FOR THEMSELVES, THEY'LL COME AFTER ME.

EXACTLY.

HAPPY LANDINGS.

SHOVE!

174

176

I HAVE A PIECE OF ADVICE FOR YOU: RUN. IF YOU STAY HERE, YOU'RE A SITTING DUCK.

AND IF I LEAVE, I'M A DEAD ONE. HERE, AT LEAST I HAVE ALEXANDER HALE WATCHING OVER ME.

LUCKY YOU. I WISH SOMEONE WAS TRYING TO KILL ME...

ANYONE WANT...PIE? I'M GONNA GO GET PIE.

OH. THAT'S WHY HE LEFT SO FAST.

I THOUGHT YOU WERE ON PROBATION.

IT'S OVER. THE PRINCIPAL CHANGED HIS MIND.

SLAM!

BECAUSE OF THIS JACKRABBIT THING?

JACKHAMMER. AND I DON'T KNOW WHY THE PRINCIPAL DOES ANYTHING...

HE'S NOT THE ONLY ONE WHO'S TOUGH TO FIGURE OUT. YESTERDAY, YOU WERE BUSTING HIS CHOPS LIKE YOU WANTED PROBATION. AND TODAY, YOU'RE FREE AS A BIRD.

YOU BUSTED THE PRINCIPAL'S CHOPS? ARE YOU PSYCHO? WHY WOULD YOU DO THAT?

YEAH, BEN. WHY WOULD YOU DO THAT?

181

WHAT WAS THAT ALL ABOUT?

JUST MY DAILY DOSE OF CHIP SCHACTER INTIMIDATION.

THIS WASN'T HIS USUAL INTIMIDATION. IT WAS DIFFERENT. LIKE, WELL...LIKE CHIP RESPECTS YOU NOW.

MUNCH MUNCH

I THINK, IN HIS OWN WAY, CHIP WAS TRYING TO BE NICE. IT'S ACTUALLY KIND OF CUTE...

CUTE?! OH NO. YOU LIKE HIM, DON'T YOU? JUST LIKE ALL THE OTHER GIRLS.

YOU KNOW HE'S A JERK BUT YOU KEEP HOPING THAT DEEP DOWN INSIDE, HE'S NICE.

AND DEEP DOWN INSIDE, YOU'RE AN IDIOT.

I DON'T LIKE CHIP.

WELL, IF YOU DO, FORGET ABOUT IT. HE AND TINA CUEVO ARE A THING.

THEY ARE?!

YOU DIDN'T KNOW? WHAT KIND OF SPIES ARE YOU?

I HAVE TO FIND ERICA...

WE NEED TO GET YOU TO A SAFE PLACE. THE ENEMY IS COMING FOR YOU.

Initiate scans

Commence vocal analysis

MY DOG HAS FLEAS.

IDENTIFICATION CONFIRMED. ALEXANDER HALE. ENTRY APPROVED.

CAN SOMEONE OPEN THE DOOR? THE ENTRY SYSTEM'S ON THE FRITZ AGAIN!

CLICK CLUNK!

THIS IS WHAT HAPPENS WHEN THE GOVERNMENT SUBCONTRACTS EVERYTHING TO THE LOWEST BIDDER.

PROFESSOR SIMON SAYS I SHOULDN'T EVEN BE ALLOWED TO USE A FORK.

OH. WELL, LET'S CONSIDER THIS A LEARNING MOMENT. IT'S ACTUALLY QUITE AN EXCITING OPPORTUNITY.

HOW?

YOU'VE BEEN HERE ONLY A FEW WEEKS AND YOU'RE ALREADY PART OF A REAL MISSION.

THERE ARE ACTUAL SPIES WHO NEVER GET TO BE PART OF ANYTHING THIS EXCITING.

THEY NEVER GET TO HAVE ASSASSINS TARGET THEM? HOW SAD.

IT IS SAD. THIS IS WHAT ESPIONAGE IS ALL ABOUT! IF YOU COME THROUGH THIS ALIVE, YOU MIGHT JUST END UP THE GOLDEN BOY AROUND HERE...

LIKE ME.

I SUPPOSE.

THAT'S THE SPIRIT!

MAKE YOURSELF AT HOME, HAVE A SNACK. REST ASSURED THAT I'M ON THE JOB.

IS THAT ONLY ONE PERSON?

THAT WE CAN SEE, WHICH MEANS THERE'S PROBABLY A DOZEN WE CAN'T.

ATTENTION. THIS IS BIG DOG. THE ENEMY IS PROCEEDING THROUGH THE SOUTHWESTERN QUADRANT TOWARD THE DORMITORY. ALL AVAILABLE AGENTS, CONVERGE THERE ON THE DOUBLE.

ALL OF YOU, COME WITH ME.

CLICK!

WAIT!

YOU'RE TAKING MY PROTECTION?

AFTER WE HANDLE THESE GUYS, YOU WON'T NEED PROTECTION ANYMORE.

SLAM!

IT REALLY LOOKS LIKE THERE'S JUST ONE GUY.

ATTACK!

CRASH!

OH NO.
NOT MIKE!

195

PFUT!

ARGHH!

CUT!

HOW ARE YOU FEELING?

GREAT, THANKS TO YOU.

CLICK!

SHHHHHH!

TCHK TCHK TCHK

RUMBLE

RUMBLE

RUMBLE

HOW DID YOU FIND ME WHEN THE CIA COULDN'T?

I NEVER LOST YOU. WHEN ALL THE AGENTS ON CAMPUS STARTED GOING ONE WAY, I WENT THE OTHER...JUST IN CASE THE BAD GUYS HAD CREATED A DIVERSION. LUCKILY, I WAS ABLE TO COMMANDEER A MOTORCYCLE TO FOLLOW THE VAN.

THE BAD GUYS DIDN'T ARRANGE THAT DIVERSION. THEY JUST GOT LUCKY. THE GUY THE CIA CAUGHT WAS MY FRIEND MIKE, FROM BACK HOME. HE WANTED TO SPRING ME FOR A PARTY TONIGHT.

AT THE EXACT MOMENT TO DISTRACT THE CIA? THAT'S SUSPICIOUS.

MIKE IS NOT THE ENEMY. I'VE KNOWN HIM SINCE KINDERGARTEN.

YOU CAN'T TRUST ANYONE.

LAID BY
ZACHARY TAYLOR,
PRESIDENT OF THE
UNITED STATES,
MAY 14, 1849

WE'RE INSIDE THE WASHINGTON MONUMENT?!

TELL ANYONE I HAVE THE KEYS AND I'LL KILL YOU.

HOW ON EARTH DO YOU HAVE THE KEYS TO THE WASHINGTON MONUMENT? DID YOUR FATHER GIVE THEM TO YOU?

DON'T BE RIDICULOUS.

MY GRANDFATHER GAVE THEM TO ME.

WHY DOES YOUR GRANDFATHER HAVE THE KEYS TO THE WASHINGTON MONUMENT?

MY FAMILY WAS GIVEN THEM RIGHT AFTER IT WAS BUILT, SEEING AS IT WAS SUCH AN IMPORTANT PART OF THE CITY'S DEFENSE SYSTEM.

DEFENSE SYSTEM?

IT'S A FIFTY-FIVE-STORY SURVEILLANCE TOWER BUILT IN THE MIDDLE OF OUR NATION'S CAPITAL ON THE EVE OF THE CIVIL WAR.

THINK THEY BUILT IT JUST FOR TOURISTS?

I'M PRETTY SURE EVERYBODY IN AMERICA THINKS THAT. EXCEPT YOU.

211

IT'S A LITTLE OUTDATED TECHNOLOGY-WISE, BUT IT'S STILL THE BEST PLACE TO CASE THE ENTIRE CITY.

THERE'S THE BAD GUYS.

SO WHAT DO WE DO NOW?

WAIT FOR THEM TO LEAVE.

THAT'S YOUR WHOLE PLAN? CAN'T YOU AT LEAST CALL YOUR FATHER AND HAVE HIM COME GET US OUT OF THIS?

HA!

YOUR FATHER ISN'T A VERY GOOD SPY, IS HE?

YOU SUSPECTED THERE MIGHT BE A DECOY. HE DIDN'T. IN FACT, HE TOOK MY ENTIRE SECURITY DETAIL, ALLOWING ME TO GET CAPTURED. YOUR FATHER TALKS A LOT ABOUT ALL THE GREAT THINGS HE'S DONE...BUT I'VE NEVER SEEN HIM DO ANYTHING GREAT.

WOW. SOMEONE FINALLY NOTICED.

YOU MEAN NO ONE ELSE KNOWS?

LIKE WHO?

THE DIRECTOR OF THE CIA.

IF THE CIA DIRECTOR KNEW MY FATHER WAS A FRAUD, THEN HE WOULDN'T HAVE ASSIGNED HIM TO PROTECT YOU. DAD HAS EVERYONE SNOWED.

WHEN DID YOU FIGURE IT OUT?

ONE DAY WHEN I WAS SIX, DAD BLEW UP OUR KITCHEN. HE'D JUST HAD MISSILES INSTALLED IN THE HEADLIGHTS OF HIS CAR. HE GOT THE CONTROLS CONFUSED, AND...NEXT THING I KNEW, OUR REFRIGERATOR WAS GOING INTO ORBIT.

FOR THE TEN MILLIONTH TIME, I AM NOT A TERRORIST. I'M A FRIEND OF BEN RIPLEY'S AND I WAS GOING TO TAKE HIM TO A PARTY...

IF YOU JUST FIND HIM, HE'LL CONFIRM IT.

HIS STORY CHECKS OUT. HE WAS JUST IN THE WRONG PLACE AT THE WRONG TIME.

OKAY. CALL HIS PARENTS AND CUT HIM LOOSE. TELL THEM THIS WAS A POLICE TRAINING EXERCISE HE STUMBLED INTO.

...AND THEN THERE WAS THE TIME HE WAS TRYING TO COMPLIMENT THE WIFE OF THE PRESIDENT OF TANZANIA, BUT HE BOTCHED HIS SWAHILI AND TOLD HER SHE SMELLED LIKE A DISEASED WILDEBEEST.

LOOKS LIKE THEY'RE ADMITTING DEFEAT. TIME TO GO.

EVERYTHING I TOLD YOU TONIGHT IS CONFIDENTIAL. TELL ANYONE...

...AND YOU'LL KILL ME. I KNOW. WHERE ARE WE GOING?

BACK TO CAMPUS.

I WAS JUST ABDUCTED FROM CAMPUS!

THAT'S WHY WE'RE GOING BACK. IF WE WANT TO FIGURE OUT WHAT'S GOING ON, THAT'S WHERE ALL THE CLUES ARE.

216

WHAT'S WRONG? SHE'S ON OUR SIDE...ISN'T SHE?

THE MOMENT THEY SEE US, THEY'LL DRAG US TO A DEBRIEFING ROOM AND GRILL US FOR THE NEXT TEN HOURS.

WE DON'T HAVE TIME FOR THAT.

ACCESSBANKING

ATM

HEY! THAT'S BEN! WITH A GIRL!

RIGHT. I SUPPOSE YOU'RE HERE TO FIND OUT HOW MUCKED UP THINGS ARE.

WAIT. THE WHOLE DODDERING PROFESSOR THING IS FAKE?

THE BEST WAY TO STAY IN THE LOOP IS TO ACT LIKE YOU'RE COMPLETELY OUT OF IT.

PEOPLE WILL SPILL GOBS OF INFORMATION RIGHT IN FRONT OF YOU. THROWS OFF YOUR ENEMIES, TOO.

SWING!

WHAT'S THE FALLOUT BACK HERE?

OH, THE POOP HAS HIT THE FAN. EVERYONE IS QUITE UPSET ABOUT YOUNG RIPLEY'S ABDUCTION—AND OUR MOLE PROBLEM.

THEY'RE THINKING ABOUT INITIATING PROJECT OMEGA.

FOR THIS?! WHY?

BECAUSE THEY'RE SCARED. THE ACADEMY HAS OBVIOUSLY BEEN COMPROMISED.

WHAT'S PROJECT OMEGA?

THE LAST-RESORT, END-OF-THE-LINE OPTION: THEY SHUT DOWN THE ACADEMY.

THEY CAN'T DO THAT! I JUST GOT HERE!

IT'S NOT SET IN STONE YET. THEY'RE HAVING A COUNCIL TO DISCUSS IT AT NOON, HERE ON CAMPUS. ALL THE HIGHER-UPS FROM THE VARIOUS INTELLIGENCE AGENCIES WILL BE GRACING US WITH THEIR PRESENCE, SEEING AS THE FATE OF THIS INSTITUTION IS THREATENED BY UNSPEAKABLE EVIL.

COOKIE?

IF THEY SHUT THIS PLACE DOWN, I'LL HAVE TO GO TO NORMAL SCHOOL...WITH NORMAL PEOPLE. IT'LL BE HORRIBLE.

THEN WE'D BEST FIGURE OUT WHO WE'RE UP AGAINST. BENJAMIN, THE PREVAILING THEORY HERE IS THAT WE'RE UP AGAINST A RENEGADE SECT OF ARABS. IS THAT WHO ABDUCTED YOU?

I DON'T THINK SO. THEY WERE LISTENING TO SPORTS RADIO IN THE VAN. IN ENGLISH.

BY THE WAY, THIS COOKIE IS AMAZING.

THANKS. MY SECRET IS I USE A PINCH OF COCONUT FLAKES.

DID YOU HEAR THEM SPEAK IN ARABIC AT ALL?

NO...ALTHOUGH I DIDN'T REALLY GET A CHANCE TO HEAR THEM SAY ANYTHING. ERICA KNOCKED THEM UNCONSCIOUS PRETTY QUICKLY.

YES, SHE TENDS TO DO THAT. SO IT SEEMS SOMEONE IS JUST TRYING TO FRAME THE ARABS...WHICH MEANS THE CHATTER THEY BROADCAST WAS A MISLEAD AS WELL.

WHY PLANT FAKE CHATTER SAYING THEY WERE COMING TO ABDUCT ME? WOULDN'T ALERTING THE CIA THAT THEY WERE COMING BE A BAD IDEA?

NOT NECESSARILY. IT ALLOWED THEM TO KNOW EXACTLY WHERE YOU WOULD BE: IN THE SECURE BUNKER.

BUT THEY'D STILL HAVE TO DEAL WITH ALL THE CIA AGENTS. THERE'S NO WAY THEY COULD HAVE KNOWN MIKE WAS GOING TO DIVERT THEM...

DO YOU STILL HAVE THAT POST-IT NOTE FROM THE VAN?

THEY DID KNOW MIKE WAS COMING. THIS IS A TIME. BUT INSTEAD OF WRITING IT IN HOURS AND MINUTES, THEY WROTE IT IN SECONDS. 70,200 SECONDS AFTER MIDNIGHT IS 7:30 P.M.

70,200

EXACTLY THE TIME YOUR FRIEND ARRIVED ON CAMPUS.

I TOLD YOU YOU CAN'T TRUST ANYONE!

THERE'S NO WAY MIKE WAS INVOLVED IN THIS! SOMEONE JUST SET HIM UP.

223

WHO?

CHIP SCHACTER.

PLEASE. THAT BOY'S A MORON.

SOMETIMES PEOPLE PRETEND TO BE DUMB TO GET OTHERS TO DROP THEIR GUARD.

TOUCHÉ.

I THINK CHIP PUT THIS IN MY JACKET POCKET AT LUNCH TODAY.

Meet me in the library at midnight. Your life depends on it.

WHY DIDN'T YOU MENTION THIS?

IT KIND OF SLIPPED MY MIND. WHAT WITH BEING KIDNAPPED BY THE ENEMY AND ALL. IT SEEMS LIKE HE'S TRYING TO LURE ME INTO A TRAP.

YOU HAVE NO PROOF OF THAT.

224

CHIP'S CONNECTED TO THE LAST BOMB UNDER THE SCHOOL. HE EITHER FOUND IT OR PLANTED IT. THAT PUTS HIM CLOSER TO THE PLOT THAN ANYONE ELSE.

AND HE'S DATING TINA CUEVO, THE ONLY STUDENT WITH ACCESS TO MY FILE.

THEY'RE DATING? HOW'D YOU KNOW THAT?

SHHHHHHH!!

THE ENEMY FOUND US!

WORSE. THE ADMINISTRATION. IF THEY CATCH YOU, OUR INVESTIGATION IS TOAST. FIND CHIP SCHACTER!

LOCK!

SWISH!

BAM!

CRACK!

227

PLEASE, NO MORE QUESTIONS! IF YOU SHOULD BE QUESTIONING ANYONE, IT'S CHIP SCHACTER!

ARE YOU TELLING ME HOW TO RUN AN OPERATION? WHY DON'T YOU LEAVE THIS TO THE PROFESSIONALS?

LAST TIME I DID THAT, I GOT KIDNAPPED.

LISTEN HERE, PIPSQUEAK...

SLAM!

AGENT HALE! WHAT BRINGS YOU HERE?

I'M TAKING BENJAMIN TO CIA HEADQUARTERS, WHERE HE CAN BE QUESTIONED WITH MORE SKILL...

AND LESS ATTITUDE.

SORRY ABOUT THESE. JUST A NECESSARY PART OF THE RUSE.

YOU'RE SPRINGING ME? WON'T YOU GET IN TROUBLE FOR THIS?

LET'S JUST SAY I OWE YOU ONE.

ACCESSBANKING

I NEED TO RETURN AND COVER YOUR TRACKS. BUT DON'T WORRY, YOU'LL BE IN GOOD HANDS.

RUMBLE

ERICA?

WELCOME BACK.

WHERE ARE YOU?

ON CAMPUS, LOOKING INTO SOME THINGS. BUT I NEED YOU TO TAIL SOMEONE FOR ME.

CHIP?

NO. TINA CUEVO. SHE'S THE MOLE...

AND SHE'S ON THE MOVE.

TINA? BUT...

SHE'S LEAVING CAMPUS RIGHT NOW. DO YOU SEE HER?

YEAH, I SEE HER.

GOOD. NOW DON'T LET HER SEE YOU.

LOOKS LIKE EVERYONE'S ARRIVING TO DISCUSS PROJECT OMEGA.

OH YEAH, IT'S A REGULAR WHO'S WHO IN ESPIONAGE HERE TODAY.

HOW DO YOU KNOW TINA'S THE MOLE?

CHIP TOLD ME. I HAD A TALK WITH HIM ABOUT WHY HE SLIPPED YOU THAT MESSAGE YESTERDAY. TURNS OUT, HE WAS COMING TO YOU FOR HELP.

ME?! WHY NOT YOU?

KRACK!

APPARENTLY, I INTIMIDATE PEOPLE. HE WAS WORRIED I'D TURN HIM IN.

FOR WHAT?

CONDUCTING AN UNAUTHORIZED INVESTIGATION. CHIP DIDN'T PLANT THAT BOMB UNDER THE SCHOOL. HE WAS TRYING TO FIGURE OUT WHO DID.

233

BUT HE TRIED TO KICK MY BUTT WHEN I SAW HIM WITH IT.

HE THOUGHT YOU MIGHT GET HIM IN TROUBLE.

BUT THEN YOU DIDN'T RAT HIM OUT TO THE PRINCIPAL. WHICH HE RESPECTED.

AND THEN HE TURNED AROUND AND RATTED OUT HIS GIRLFRIEND TO YOU?

YOUR SOURCE GOT THINGS WRONG. CHIP HASN'T BEEN DATING TINA. HE'S BEEN INVESTIGATING HER.

234

WHOA!

IT'S ME! I JUST WANTED TO TALK.

DID YOU JUST TAIL ME FROM CAMPUS?

YEAH. BECAUSE WHEN I TRIED TO SEE YOU ON CAMPUS LAST NIGHT, I GOT DOGPILED BY THE GOON SQUAD.

BEN, YOU'RE ON A COVERT OP. YOU NEED TO DITCH THIS GUY.

I KNOW.

YOU KNEW ABOUT THAT? WHY DIDN'T YOU TRY TO PROTECT ME? OR WARN ME ABOUT THEM? I NEARLY GOT KILLED...

I'M SORRY ABOUT THAT...

WHAT PART OF "DITCH THIS GUY" DID YOU NOT UNDERSTAND?

...AND THEN YOU BLEW ME OFF LAST NIGHT TOO!

LAST NIGHT? WHEN?

RIGHT OUTSIDE YOUR SCHOOL! YOU WERE WITH A GIRL. I YELLED TO YOU, BUT YOU DIDN'T EVEN RESPOND.

THAT'S HOW THE GUARDS KNEW WE WERE BACK! THIS YAHOO TIPPED THEM OFF!

MIKE, I DIDN'T EVEN HEAR YOU. I SWEAR.

ALL RIGHT. I GUESS I CAN UNDERSTAND WHY THAT GIRL WOULD COMMAND YOUR ATTENTION. SHE WAS GORGEOUS. WAS THAT ERICA?

HOW DOES HE KNOW MY NAME?

HOW DO YOU KNOW HER NAME?

YOU TOLD ME, REMEMBER? A FEW WEEKS AGO. YOU BRAGGED THAT SOME HOT GIRL NAMED ERICA HAD SNUCK INTO YOUR ROOM AFTER CURFEW.

YOU TOLD HIM ABOUT THAT?

IT WASN'T A ROMANTIC THING! SHE ONLY WANTED TO WORK ON A PROJECT TOGETHER.

THAT'S NOT HOW YOU MADE IT SOUND THEN. AND IT'S NOT HOW IT LOOKS, EITHER. THE TWO OF YOU WERE SNEAKING OFF CAMPUS TOGETHER! BEN, OWN THIS!

BEN, WE NEED TO TALK.

MIKE, I'M NOT SEEING ERICA.

OH, NOW YOU'RE LYING TO ME?

EVER SINCE YOU STARTED AT THIS STUPID SCHOOL, YOU'VE BEEN A TOTAL JERK.

NO I HAVEN'T!

YOU HAVEN'T COME BACK TO SEE ME, YOU NEVER CALL, YOU TOLD ME TO COME SPRING YOU LAST NIGHT AND THEN ABANDONED ME WHEN I GOT INTO TROUBLE FOR IT...

I DIDN'T TELL YOU TO SPRING ME.

OH REALLY? WHAT DO YOU CALL THIS?

SLAM!

BEN? WHAT'S GOING ON THERE? WHERE'S TINA?

THERE YOU GO.

COLD HARD PROOF THAT YOU TEXTED ME, YOU JERK.

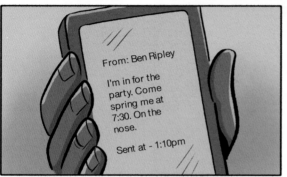

From: Ben Ripley

I'm in for the party. Come spring me at 7:30. On the nose.

Sent at - 1:10pm

MIKE...I DIDN'T SEND THIS... BUT I KNOW WHO DID.

YOU'RE SAYING YOU DIDN'T SEND THIS—EVEN THOUGH IT'S FROM YOUR PHONE?

YES! I HAVE TO GO. I'M SORRY. I PROMISE, I'LL MAKE THIS UP TO YOU. YOU'RE MY BEST FRIEND. THAT'S MORE IMPORTANT TO ME THAN ANYTHING.

239

SHOVE!

SO DO I.
IT'S TINA.

FURNACE
ROOM

NO IT ISN'T! TINA'S BEEN FRAMED!

CRASH!

CRACK!

ERICA? ARE YOU THERE?

TELL ANYONE ABOUT THIS AND I'LL HAVE TO KILL YOU.

SPY SCHOOL CONFERENCE ROOM

ERICA! WHERE ARE YOU?

..BEEP..........BEEP..........BEEP..

..BEEP..........BEEP..........BEEP..

FLASH
FLASH

BEEP..........BEEP..........BEEP..........

IT'S ALSO A HOMING DEVICE...

SPIN!

BEEP...BEEP...BEEP...BEEP...BEEP

BEEP...BEEP...BEEP...BEEP...BEEP...BEEP...BEEP...BEEP...BEEP...BEEP...BEEP...BEEP...BEEP

BEEP.BEEP.BEEP.BEEP.BEEP.BEEP.BEEP.BEEP.BEEEEEEEEEEEEEEEEEEEEEEEEEEEEEEEEEEEEEEEEEEEP.

FURNACE
ROOM

FURNACE
ROOM

E'

CRACK!

243

I WOULDN'T DO THAT IF I WERE YOU.

SPIN!

IF YOU KNOCK ME OUT, I DROP THIS— AND WE GO KABLOOEY.

TURN OFF THE BOMB.

I'LL PASS. BUT YOU KNOW WHAT I'D BE HAPPY TO DO? GET THE HECK AWAY FROM HERE BEFORE THIS GOES OFF...

C'MON, I'LL BUY YOU AN ICE CREAM.

YOU'RE NOT GOING ANYWHERE!

FLAMETHROWER BEATS STICK. YOU LOSE.

WHY DO YOU HAVE A FLAME-THROWER??

MY AIM STINKS WITH MOST WEAPONS. BUT WITH THIS, I DON'T HAVE TO WORRY ABOUT BEING ACCURATE. MAKE ONE FALSE MOVE AND I'LL FRICASSEE YOUR BUTT.

Toss!

NOW, THERE'S NO NEED TO GET UPSET. IF I WANTED TO FLAMBÉ YOU, I'D HAVE DONE IT ALREADY.

THEN WHY HAVEN'T YOU?

I HAVE A BUSINESS PROPOSITION FOR YOU. THOUGH I'D REALLY LIKE TO DISCUSS IT SOMEWHERE FAR FROM THIS BOMB. I WASN'T KIDDING ABOUT THAT ICE CREAM.

I'M NOT GOING ANYWHERE WITH YOU.

I'M PAYING. YOU CAN EVEN GET SPRINKLES.

THE LAST TIME YOU OFFERED TO GET ME DESSERT, IT WAS A RUSE TO ARRANGE MY ABDUCTION.

YESTERDAY, WHEN YOU WENT TO GET PIE, YOU STOLE MY PHONE...

TEXTED MIKE WHAT TIME TO INFILTRATE THE SCHOOL...

TAP TAP TAP!

AND THEN ERASED THE TEXT FROM MY OWN PHONE.

To:Mike Brezinski

I'm in for the party. Come spring me at 7:30. On the nose.

Sent at - 1:10pm

Delete

I KNEW YOU WERE SMART! DID YOU ALSO FIGURE OUT OUR EVIL SCHEME?

YOU'VE BEEN PLAYING THE CIA ALL ALONG, LETTING THEM KNOW THERE'S A MOLE, SENDING AN ASSASSIN TO CAMPUS, KIDNAPPING ME...

ALL TO CREATE A PANIC AND TRIGGER PROJECT OMEGA...

IT'S THE ONLY THING THAT WOULD BRING THE HEADS OF ALL THE INTELLIGENCE AGENCIES TOGETHER HERE AT ONCE. WHICH IS THE PERFECT OPPORTUNITY TO TAKE THEM ALL OUT.

MEANWHILE, YOU TOLD ME CHIP WAS SEEING TINA, WHEN IN REALITY YOU WERE THE ONE USING HER.

YOU HAVEN'T TANKED YOUR CLASSES SO YOU CAN GET A DESK JOB. YOU DID IT TO GET TUTORED BY TINA.

BUT WHEN CHIP, OF ALL PEOPLE, STUMBLED ONTO YOUR PLOT, YOU DEFLECTED HIS ATTENTION TO TINA HERSELF.

CLASSIFIED

RIPLEY, BENJAMIN

D.O.B:
Address:

249

I ADMIT, THAT WAS A LITTLE SLOPPY. BUT IT'S NOT EASY TO SNEAK THIS MUCH EXPLOSIVE INTO A CIA FACILITY. MAN, I CAN SEE WHY MY BOSSES WANT TO RECRUIT YOU. YOU HAVE BRAINS TO SPARE.

THAT'S YOUR BUSINESS PROPOSAL? YOU WANT ME TO BE A DOUBLE AGENT?

YES! IT PAYS GREAT—AND IT'S MUCH LESS DANGEROUS THAN BEING A SINGLE AGENT.

WHO DO YOU WORK FOR? THE RUSSIANS? THE SAUDIS? JIHADISTS?

NO. I WORK FOR AN INDEPENDENT CONSORTIUM OF BAD GUYS WHO CAUSE CHAOS AND MAYHEM FOR A PRICE.

WE'RE CALLED **SPYDER.**

WHY?

BECAUSE IT SOUNDS COOL. AND "AN INTERNATIONAL CONSORTIUM OF BAD GUYS WHO CAUSE CHAOS AND MAYHEM FOR A PRICE" IS A MOUTHFUL.

SO...YOU'RE EVIL SUBCONTRACTORS? DO YOU EVEN KNOW WHO'S PAYING YOU TO BUILD THIS BOMB?

NOPE! WHAT'S IT MATTER, AS LONG AS THE CHECKS CLEAR? I KNOW YOU THINK I'M A SELFISH JERK, BUT HONESTLY, AM I WORSE THAN THE CIA? THEY USED YOU AS BAIT TO CATCH THE ENEMY!

YOU'RE THE ENEMY!

AND WE NEVER KILLED YOU, EVEN WHEN WE HAD THE CHANCE. WE'LL GET RICH AND RETIRE TO PRIVATE ISLANDS BY THE TIME WE'RE FORTY! HOW'S THAT SOUND?

PRETTY GOOD, ACTUALLY.

REALLY?

REALLY. THE CIA HAS TREATED ME LIKE GARBAGE. I'VE BEEN...

HUMILIATED

BULLIED

BERATED

ABDUCTED

LOCKED IN THE BOX

AND ATTACKED BY NINJAS

HONESTLY, THIS PLACE STINKS. SO LET'S DO THIS DOUBLE-AGENT THING. WHERE DO I SIGN UP?

YOU HAVE MADE A VERY GOOD CHOICE, MY FRIEND. LET'S GO GRAB A SUNDAE AND WATCH THE FIREWORKS.

RATTLE! RATTLE!

WAKE UP! WE'RE LOCKED IN HERE WITH A BOMB! IF YOU DON'T HELP ME DEFUSE IT, WE ARE GOING TO DIE!!!!

SHAKE SHAKE!

URRGH

OH MAN, WHAT DO I DO? I'M FLUNKING BOMB DEFUSION! I DON'T WANT TO BE DEAD! I...

0:15

MURRAY SAID EVERYONE WAS GOING TO THINK I WAS A DEAD DOUBLE AGENT. WHY WOULD HE...?

HE USED MY OWN ALARM CLOCK TO FRAME ME. THAT JERK!

0:11

HE USED MY OWN ALARM CLOCK! MY ALARM CLOCK IS A PIECE OF JUNK!

BASH!

0:03

0:00

I DID IT! YES! I'M NOT DEAD!

WHAT'S GOING ON?

NOW YOU'RE CONSCIOUS? YOU COULDN'T HAVE COME TO FIVE MINUTES AGO?

YOU STOPPED THE BOMB? NICE WORK.

DID HE TRY TO KILL YOU?

FLASH! FLASH!

NO. HE OFFERED ME A JOB WITH SPYDER.

SPYDER?

THAT'S INTERESTING. WATCH OUT.

CLICK!

BOOM!

SPYDER HAS ONLY BEEN A RUMOR FOR YEARS. IF MURRAY REALLY WORKS FOR THEM, THAT'S THE FIRST PROOF WE'LL EVER HAVE IT EXISTS. WE NEED TO CATCH HIM BEFORE HE ESCAPES.

WE?

YOU MEAN, YOU WANT MY HELP?

I'D SAY YOU'VE PROVEN YOURSELF. NOW, WE JUST NEED TO FIGURE OUT WHICH WAY MURRAY WENT.

I KNOW HOW TO DO THAT. CAN I BORROW YOUR PHONE?

RING RING

SMOKESCREEN! WHERE HAVE YOU BEEN?

FINDING THE MOLE. IT'S MURRAY!

WASHOUT? NO WAY. HE'S WAY TOO LAZY FOR THAT.

IT'S A FRONT! HE JUST TRIED TO BLOW UP THE OMEGA CONFERENCE AND NOW HE'S ON THE RUN. DO YOU KNOW WHERE HE IS?

NO, BUT I CAN FIND OUT.

HAS ANYONE HERE SEEN MURRAY HILL? IT'S AN EMERGENCY!

LET'S GO GET HIM.

THIS IS ONLY A PAINTBALL GUN.

STILL LOOKS LIKE A REAL ONE. MAYBE MURRAY WON'T NOTICE.

HEY! YOU CAN'T TAKE THOSE WITHOUT PERMISSION!

WE'RE ON A MOLE HUNT. WANT TO COME?

REALLY? AWESOME!

MOBILIZE EVERYONE YOU CAN. WE NEED TO CATCH MURRAY BEFORE HE ESCAPES.

ALREADY MOBILIZING.

ANYONE ELSE YOU WANT TO INVITE? YOUR GRANDMOTHER, MAYBE?

THIS CAMPUS IS 192 SQUARE ACRES. TO FIND MURRAY, WE NEED AS MUCH HELP AS WE CAN GET.

ROAR!

YEAH, JUST STUCK.

HAUSER TOLD ME YOU HAVE THE MOLE ON THE RUN. IT'S TINA, RIGHT?

CRACK

NO, IT'S MURRAY. HE SET TINA UP.

MURRAY HILL? NO WAY. THAT GUY'S THE BIGGEST SLACKER AT SCHOOL!

NO.

HE'S A MASTER OF DIVERSION...

SO IF WE THINK HE'S HEADING FOR THE WALL, THEN THAT'S PROBABLY THE LAST THING HE'S DOING.

THIS WAY!!

THUD!

269

274

NICE WORK, HOTSHOT.

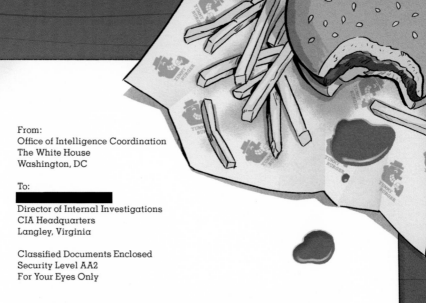

From:
Office of Intelligence Coordination
The White House
Washington, DC

To:
████████
Director of Internal Investigations
CIA Headquarters
Langley, Virginia

Classified Documents Enclosed
Security Level AA2
For Your Eyes Only

After reading the enclosed transcript, it is evident that considerable work lies ahead of us. It appears that reevaluation of ████████ ██████████, the governance of the Academy of Espionage and the CIA itself is in order. It is shocking and dismaying that the only person in the entire intelligence community to uncover direct evidence of SPYDER is a first year at the academy. Worse, a first year who didn't even officially qualify for entry. Immediate further investigation into this nefarious organization must proceed at all costs.

To that end, I recommend Benjamin Ripley's acceptance into the school be made official. He has certainly earned it. As he remains a target for SPYDER, he should be given K-24 security status—although at this time, it is probably too early to brief him on Operation Enduring Assault. If he knew that ████████████████, he'd probably flip out. Instead, allow him to once again believe he is a normal student at the academy whose life is not in the slightest bit of danger.

In addition, as far as the investigation of SPYDER is concerned, I recommend immediate activation of ████████████, aka Klondike. I am fully aware of the inherent dangers in doing so, but desperate times call for desperate measures. If SPYDER is not neutralized soon, this could portend the end of the intelligence community—and perhaps even the United States of America—as we know it.

My best to Betty and the kids.

████████████
Director of Covert Affairs

Acknowledgments

I had never published a graphic novel before, but the idea of doing one became increasingly exciting over the years. The process worked out even better than I had hoped.

The main reason for this is Anjan Sarkar, whose work on this project has exceeded my wildest dreams. His illustrations, his layout, his humor, and his attention to detail have all been amazing. Then, Lucy Ruth Cummins did a wonderful job overseeing the project. Lucy is the artistic genius who has created all of my book covers, so of course she was the perfect person to handle the graphic novel. Also, thanks are due to Justin Chanda, my publisher, who made this whole thing happen, and Krista Vitola, my editor.

Then there's the rest of my awesome team at Simon & Schuster: Erin Toller, Beth Parker, Roberta Stout, Kendra Levin, Catherine Laudone, Anne Zafian, Lisa Moraleda, Jenica Nasworthy, Tom Daly, Chava Wolin, Chrissy Noh, Anna Jarzab, Brian Murray, Devin MacDonald, Christina Pecorale, Victor Iannone, Emily Hutton, Emily Ritter, and Theresa Pang. And massive thanks to my wonderful agent, Jennifer Joel, for making my entire book career possible.

Thanks to the home team: Ronald and Jane Gibbs; Suz, Darragh, and Ciara Howard; Barry and Carole Patmore; Megan Vicente; and Georgia Simon.

And, of course, thanks to my children, Dashiell and Violet, who had been asking me when I was going to do a graphic novel for years. Here it is, kids. I hope you love it as much as I do.

Agent: Ben Ripley, age 12

Mission: Survive the "science school" that is really a front for training junior CIA operatives. And try to get the girl.

Objectives:

1. Find the devious double agent who has infiltrated the school.

...e that you are capable of being a spy, save the day, and try not to look like a fool while doing it.

DESTROY THIS NOTE ONCE YOU'VE MEMORIZED IT.

FOLLOW BEN AT THE ACADEMY OF ESPIONAGE AS HE LEARNS THE TRICKS OF THE TRADE, WITHOUT GETTING HIMSELF KILLED, IN ACTION-PACKED FULL-COLOR PANELS.

VISIT US AT SIMONANDSCHUSTER.COM/KIDS

ISBN 978-1-5344-5542-9 $12.99 U.S./$16.99 Can.

Cover illustration © 2022 by Anjan Sarkar
Cover design by Lucy Ruth Cummins
© 2022 by Simon & Schuster, Inc.
Manufactured in China
Simon & Schuster Books for Young Readers
Simon & Schuster · New York
Ages 8–12 · 0222
EBOOK EDITION ALSO AVAILABLE

STUARTGIBBS.COM
VISIT SIMONANDSCHUSTER.NET FOR A FREE READING GROUP GUIDE.